A BOOK IS A PRESENT

YOU CAN OPEN AGAIN AND AGAIN

© Mary Engelbreit

ROBERT BENCHLEY

A GOOD OLD-FASHIONED CHRISTMAS

Drawings by Gluyas Williams

The Ipswich Press
Ipswich, Massachusetts 01938

COPYRIGHT ACKNOWLEDGEMENTS

From THE BENCHLEY ROUNDUP by Robert Benchley, illustrations by Gluyas Williams:
"Christmas Afternoon," Copyright, 1921, by Harper & Row, Publishers, Inc.; renewed, 1949, by Gertrude D. Benchley.
"Uncle Edith's Ghost Story," Copyright, 1927, by Harper & Row, Publishers, Inc.; renewed, 1955, by Gertrude D. Benchley.
"Editha's Christmas Burglar," Copyright, 1925, by Harper & Row, Publishers, Inc.; renewed, 1953, by Gertrude D. Benchley.
"Another Uncle Edith Christmas Story," Copyright, 1930, by Robert C. Benchley; renewed, 1958, by Gertrude D. Benchley.
"The Stranger Within Our Gates," Copyright, 1930, by Robert C. Benchley; renewed, 1958, by Gertrude D. Benchley.
"The King and the Old Man," Copyright, 1932, by Robert C. Benchley; renewed, 1960, by Gertrude D. Benchley.

From PLUCK AND LUCK by Robert Benchley, illustrations by Gluyas Williams:
"A Christmas Pantomime," Copyright, 1925, by Harper & Row, Publishers, Inc.; renewed, 1953, by Gertrude D. Benchley.
"The Young Folks' Day," Copyright, 1925, by Harper & Row, Publishers, Inc.; renewed, 1953, by Gertrude D. Benchley.
"Here Come the Children," Copyright, 1925, by Harper & Row, Publishers, Inc.; renewed, 1953, by Gertrude D. Benchley.
"Holiday! Holiday!," Copyright, 1925, by Harper & Row, Publishers, Inc.; renewed, 1953, by Gertrude D. Benchley.

From AFTER 1903—WHAT? by Robert Benchley:
"A New Day," Copyright, 1938, by Robert C. Benchley; renewed, 1966, by Gertrude D. Benchley.

From CHIPS OFF THE OLD BENCHLEY by Robert Benchley, illustrations by Gluyas Williams:
"Bayeux Christmas Presents Early," Copyright, 1949, 1977 by Gertrude D. Benchley.
" 'Greetings From—' ", Copyright, 1949, 1977 by Gertrude D. Benchley.

From THE EARLY WORM by Robert Benchley, illustrations by Gluyas Williams:
"A Good Old-Fashioned Christmas," Copyright, 1927, by Harper & Row, Publishers, Inc.; renewed, 1955, by Gertrude D. Benchley.
"At Last a Substitute for Snow," Copyright, 1927, by Harper & Row, Publishers, Inc.; renewed, 1955, by Gertrude D. Benchley.
"The Rise and Fall of the Christmas Card," Copyright, 1927, by Harper & Row, Publishers, Inc.; renewed 1955, by Gertrude D. Benchley.

From LOVE CONQUERS ALL by Robert Benchley, illustrations by Gluyas Williams:
"A Christmas Spectacle," Copyright, 1922, by Harper & Row, Publishers, Inc.; renewed, 1950, by Gertrude D. Benchley.
"Home for the Holidays," Copyright, 1922, by Harper & Row, Publishers, Inc.; renewed, 1950, by Gertrude D. Benchley.

Reprinted by permission of Harper & Row, Publishers, Inc.

Contents

Foreword 7
A Good Old-Fashioned Christmas 9
The Rise and Fall of the Christmas Card 20
"Greetings from —" 26
The Stranger Within Our Gates 32 *also in The Benchley Roundup*
Bayeux Christmas Presents Early 36
Here Come the Children 38
Another Uncle Edith Christmas Story 41 *also in The Benchley Roundup*
Home for the Holidays 46
Holiday! Holiday! 52
A Christmas Spectacle 55
The King and the Old Man 61 *also in The Benchley Roundup*
A Christmas Pantomime 64
Editha's Christmas Burglar 69 *also in The Benchley Roundup*
The Young Folks' Day 74
Christmas Afternoon 78 *also in The Benchley Roundup*
Uncle Edith's Ghost Story 83 *also in The Benchley Roundup*
At Last a Substitute for Snow 88
A New Day 93

Foreword

ROBERT BENCHLEY may well be the funniest American writer since Mark Twain. In this collection of eighteen sparkling gems—never before brought together in one volume—he turns his attention to that perennial and intractable problem: how to cope with the holiday season.

For confirmed Benchley fans, here is an occasion for a joyful reunion with the master; for the rest of you, a chance to make the acquaintance of one of our best-loved humorists.

Robert Benchley once supplied this modest autobiographical sketch to *Current Biography:* "Born on the Isle of Wight, September 15, 1807, shipped as cabin boy on the *Florence J. Marble* in 1815, wrote *A Tale of Two Cities* in 1820, married Princess Anastasie of Portugal in 1831 (children: Prince Rupprecht and several little girls), buried in Westminster Abbey in 1871." As the editors had to point out, this was not strictly true.

Benchley was in fact born in Worcester, Massachusetts, in 1889. He graduated in 1912 from Harvard College, where he was president of the *Lampoon.* His work in the years that followed displayed a remarkable range of talents. He was associate editor of the New York *Tribune* Sunday magazine, secretary to the Aircraft Board in Washington during

World War I, managing editor of *Vanity Fair*, dramatic editor of the old *Life* magazine, contributing columnist for the New York *World*, drama and press critic for *The New Yorker*, author of a dozen books of humorous essays, actor in forty-six short films and several feature-length ones, and an occasional radio performer. A host of friends, as well as countless admirers who felt he was their friend, were saddened by his untimely passing in 1945.

Three things combined to give people the uncanny feeling that they knew Robert Benchley personally: the disarmingly direct style of his writing, the engaging expressiveness of his face on the movie screen, and the illustrations which GLUYAS WILLIAMS created for his books. Indeed, when a telling line of Benchley's comes to mind, it is accompanied as often as not by a deft Williams portrait of our bemused protagonist.

Williams, who was born in San Francisco in 1888, was in the class ahead of Benchley at Harvard and was his colleague on the *Lampoon*. After a stint as an art student in Paris, he embarked on a career as a cartoonist and illustrator that would eventually bring him renown throughout the English-speaking world. During Williams' most prolific years, his cartoons were seen by an estimated five million readers of more than seventy newspapers, from California to South Africa, by way of Boston and London. In 1946, the Boston Museum of Fine Arts presented an exhibition of one hundred of his original drawings.

Gluyas Williams lived for many years in the Boston suburb of Newton, where he died in February 1982.

A Good Old-Fashioned Christmas

SOONER or later at every Christmas party, just as things are beginning to get good, someone shuts his eyes, puts his head back and moans softly: "Ah, well, this isn't like the good old days. We don't seem to have any good old-fashioned Christmases any more." To which the answer from my corner of the room is: "All right! That suits me!"

Just what they have in mind when they say "old-fashioned Christmas" you never can pin them down to telling. "Lots of snow," they mutter, "and lots of food." Yet, if you work it right, you can still get plenty of snow and food today. Snow, at any rate.

Then there seems to be some idea of the old-fashioned Christmas being, of necessity, in the country. It doesn't make any difference whether you were raised on a farm or whether your ideas of a rural Christmas were gleaned from pictures in old copies of "Harper's Young People," you must give folks to understand that such were the surroundings in which you spent your childhood holidays. And that, ah, me, those days will never come again!

Well, supposing you get your wish some time. Supposing, let us say, your wife's folks who live up in East Russet

Vermont, write and ask you to come up and bring the children for a good old-fashioned Christmas, "while we are all still together," they add cheerily with their flair for putting everybody in good humor.

Hurray, hurray! Off to the country for Christmas! Pack up all the warm clothes in the house, for you will need them up there where the air is clean and cold. Snow-shoes? Yes, put them in, or better yet, Daddy will carry them. What fun! Take along some sleigh bells to jangle in case there aren't enough on the pung. There must be jangling sleigh-bells. And whisky for frost-bite. Or is it snake-bite that whisky is for? Anyway, put it in! We're off! Good-by all! Good-by! JANGLE-JANGLE-JANGLE-Jangle-Jangle-Jangle-jangle-jangle-jangle-jangle-jangle-jangle!

In order to get to East Russet you take the Vermont Central as far as Twitchell's Falls and change there for Torpid River Junction, where a spur line takes you right into Gormley. At Gormley you are met by a buckboard which takes you back to Torpid River Junction again. By this time a train or something has come in which will wait for the local from Besus. While waiting for this you will have time to send your little boy to school, so that he can finish the third grade.

At East Russet Grandpa meets you with the sleigh. The bags are piled in and Mother sits in front with Lester in her lap while Daddy takes Junior and Ga-Ga in back with him and the luggage. Giddap, Esther Girl!

Esther Girl giddaps, and two suitcases fall out. Heigh-ho! Out we get to pick them up, brushing the snow off and filling our cuffs with it as we do so. After all, there is nothing like snow for getting up one's cuffs. Good clean snow never hurt anyone. Which is lucky, because after you

Esther Girl giddaps,
and two suitcases fall out.

have gone a mile or so, you discover that Ga-Ga is miss-
ing. Never mind, she is a self-reliant little girl and will
doubtless find her way to the farm by herself. Probably she
will be there waiting for you when you arrive.

The farm is situated on a hill about eleven hundred miles
from the center of town, just before you get into Canada.
If there is a breeze in winter, they get it. But what do
they care for breezes, so long as they have the Little Colo-
nel oil-heater in the front room, to make everything cozy
and warm within a radius of four inches! And the big open
fireplace with the draught coming down it! Fun for everybody!

You are just driving up to the farmhouse in the sleigh,
with the entire right leg frozen where the lap robe has
slipped out. Grandma is waiting for you at the door and
you bustle in, all glowing with good cheer. "Merry
Christmas, Grandma!" Lester is cross and Junior is asleep
and has to be dragged by the hand upstairs, bumping
against each step all the way. It is so late that you decide
that you all might as well go to bed, especially as you
learn that breakfast is at four-thirty. It usually is at four,
but Christmas being a holiday everyone sleeps late.

As you reach the top of the stairs you get into a current
of cold air which has something of the quality of the temperature in a nice well-regulated crypt. This is the Bed
Room Zone, and in it the thermometer never tops the zero
mark from October fifteenth until the middle of May.
Those rooms in which no one sleeps are used to store per-
ishable vegetables in, and someone has to keep thumbing
the tomatoes and pears every so often to prevent their getting so hard that they crack.

The way to get undressed for bed in one of Grandpa's
bedrooms is as follows: Starting from the foot of the stairs

where it is warm, run up two at a time to keep the circulation going as long as possible. Opening the bedroom door with one hand, tear down the curtains from the window with the other, pick up the rugs from the floor and snatch the spread from the top of the bureau. Pile all these on the bed, cover with the closet door which you have wrenched from its hinges, and leap quickly underneath. It sometimes helps to put on a pair of rubbers over your shoes.

And even when you are in bed, you have no guarantee of going to sleep. Grandpa's mattresses seem to contain the overflow from the silo, cornhusks, baked-potato skins and long, stringy affairs which feel like pipe cleaners. On a cold night, snuggling down into these is about like snuggling down into a bed of damp pine cones out in the forest.

Then there are Things abroad in the house. Shortly after you get into bed, the stairs start snapping. Next something runs along the roof over your head. You say to yourself: "Don't be silly. It's only Santa Claus." Then it runs along the wall behind the head of the bed. Santa Claus wouldn't do that. Down the long hall which leads into the ell of the house you can hear the wind sighing softly, with an occasional reassuring bang of a door.

The unmistakable sound of someone dying in great pain rises from just below the window-sill. It is a sort of low moan, with just a touch of strangulation in it. Perhaps Santa has fallen off the roof. Perhaps that story you once heard about Grandpa's house having been a hang-out for Revolutionary smugglers is true, and one of the smugglers has come back for his umbrella. The only place at a time like this is down under the bedclothes. But the children are frightened and demand to be taken home, and Grandpa has to be called to explain that it is only Blue Bell out in the barn. Blue Bell has asthma, and on a cold night they have to be very patient with her.

Christmas morning dawns cloudy and cold, with the threat of plenty more snow, and, after all, what would Christmas be without snow? You lie in bed for one hour and a quarter trying to figure out how you can get up without losing the covers from around you. A glance at the water pitcher shows that it is time for them to put the red

The entire family enters, purple and chattering and exceedingly cross.

ball up for skating. You think of the nice warm bathroom at home, and decide that you can wait until you get back there before shaving.

This breaking the ice in the pitcher seems to be a feature of the early lives of all great men which they look back on with tremendous satisfaction. "When I was a boy, I used to have to break the ice in the pitcher every morning before I could wash," is said with as much pride as one might say, "When I was a boy I stood at the head of my class." Just what virtue there is in having to break ice in a pitcher is not evident, unless it lies in their taking the bother to break the ice and wash at all. Any time that I have to break ice in a pitcher as preliminary to washing, I go unwashed, that's all. And Benjamin Franklin and U.S. Grant and Rutherford B. Hayes can laugh as much as they like. I'm nobody's fool about a thing like that.

Getting the children dressed is a lot of fun when you have to keep pumping their limbs up and down to keep them from freezing out stiff. The children love it and are just as bright and merry as little pixies when it is time to go downstairs and say "Good morning" to Grandpa and Grandma. The entire family enters the dining-room purple and chattering and exceedingly cross.

After breakfast everyone begins getting dinner. The kitchen being the only warm place in the house may have something to do with it. But before long there are so many potato peelings and turkey feathers and squash seeds and floating bits of pie crust in the kitchen that the women-folk send you and the children off into the front part of the house to amuse yourselves and get out of the way.

Then what a jolly time you and the kiddies and Grandpa have together! You can either slide on the horse-hair sofa, or play "The Wayside Chapel" on the piano (the piano has scroll-work on either side of the music rack with yellow silk showing through), or look out the window and see ten miles of dark gray snow. Perhaps you may even go out to the barn and look at the horses and cows, but really, as you walk down between the stalls, when you have seen one horse or one cow you have seen them all. And besides, the cold in the barn has an added flavor of damp harness leather and musty carriage upholstery which eats into your very marrow.

Of course, there are the presents to be distributed, but that takes on much the same aspect as the same ceremony in the new-fashioned Christmas, except that in the really old-fashioned Christmas the presents weren't so tricky. Children got mostly mittens and shoes, with a sled thrown in sometimes for dissipation. Where a boy today is bored by three o'clock in the afternoon with his electric grain-elevator and miniature pond with real perch in it, the old-fashioned boy was lucky if he got a copy of "Naval Battles of the War of 1812" and an orange. Now this feature is often brought up in praise of the old way of doing things. "I tell you," says Uncle Gyp, "the children in my time never got such presents as you get today." And he seems proud of the fact, as if there were some virtue accruing to him for it. If the children of today can get electric grain-elevators and tin automobiles for Christmas, why aren't they that much better off than their grandfathers who got only wristlets? Learning the value of money, which seems to be the only argument of the stand-patters, doesn't hold very much water as a Christmas slogan. The value of money can be learned in just about five minutes when the time comes, but Christmas is not the season.

But to return to the farm, where you and the kiddies and Gramp' are killing time. You can either bring in wood from the woodshed, or thaw out the pump, or read books in the bookcase over the writing-desk. Of the three, bringing in the wood will probably be the most fun, as you are likely to burn yourself thawing out the pump, and the list of reading matter on hand includes "The Life and Deeds of General Grant," "Our First Century," "Andy's Trip to Portland," bound volumes of the Jersey Cattle Breeders' Gazette and "Diseases of the Horse." Then there are some old copies of "Round the Lamp" for the years 1850-54 and some colored plates showing plans for the approaching World's Fair at Chicago.

Thus the time passes, in one round of gayety after another, until you are summoned to dinner. Here all caviling

Then you sit and moan.

must cease. The dinner lives up to the advertising. If an old-fashioned Christmas could consist entirely of dinner without the old-fashioned bedrooms, the old-fashioned water pitcher, and the old-fashioned entertainments, we professional pessimists wouldn't have a turkey leg to stand on. But, as has been pointed out, it is possible to get a good dinner without going up to East Russet, Vt., or, if it isn't, then our civilization has been a failure.

And the dinner only makes the aftermath seem worse. According to an old custom of the human race, everyone overeats. Deliberately and with considerable gusto you sit at the table and say pleasantly: "My, but I won't be able to walk after this. Just a little more dark meat, please, Grandpa, and just a dab of stuffing. Oh, dear, that's too much!" You haven't the excuse of the drunkard, who becomes oblivious to his excesses after several drinks. You know what you are doing, and yet you make light of it and even laugh about is as long as you *can* laugh without splitting out a seam.

And then you sit and moan. If you were having a good new-fashioned Christmas, you could go out to the movies or take a walk, or a ride, but to be really old-fashioned you must stick close to the house, for in the old days there were no movies and no automobiles and if you wanted to take a walk you had to have the hired man go ahead of you with a snow-shovel and make a tunnel. There are probably plenty of things to do in the country today, and just as many automobiles and electric lights as there are in the city, but you can't call Christmas with all these improvements "an old-fashioned Christmas." That's cheating.

If you are going through with the thing right, you have got to retire to the sitting-room after dinner and *sit*. Of course, you can go out and play in the snow if you want to, but you know as well as I do that this playing in the snow is all right when you are small but a bit trying on anyone over thirty. And anyway, it always began to snow along about three in the afternoon an old-fashioned Christmas day, with a cheery old leaden sky overhead and a jolly old gale sweeping around the corners of the house.

No, you simply must sit indoors, in front of a fire if you insist, but nevertheless with nothing much to do. The children are sleepy and snarling. Grandpa is just sleepy. Someone tries to start the conversation, but everyone else is too gorged with food to be able to move the lower jaw sufficiently to articulate. It develops that the family is in possession of the loudest-ticking clock in the world and along about four o'clock it begins to break its own record. A stenographic report of the proceedings would read as follows:

"Ho-Hum! I'm sleepy! I shouldn't have eaten so much."
"Tick-tock-tick-tock-tick-tock-tick-tock—"
"It seems just like Sunday, doesn't it?"
"Look at Grandpa! He's asleep."
"Here, Junior! Don't plague Grandpa. Let him sleep."
"Tick-tock-tick-tock-tick-tock—"
"Junior! Let Grandpa alone! Do you want Mamma to take you upstairs?"
"Ho-hum!"
"Tick-tock-tick-tock-tick-tock—"

Louder and louder the clock ticks, until something snaps in your brain and you give a sudden leap into the air with a scream, finally descending to strangle each of the family in turn, and Grandpa as he sleeps. Then, as you feel your end is near, all the warm things you have ever known come back to you, in a flash. You remember the hot Sunday subway to Coney, your trip to Mexico, the bull-fighters of Spain.

You dash out into the snowdrifts and plunge along until you sink exhausted. Only the fact that this article ends here keeps you from freezing to death, with an obituary the next day reading:

"DIED suddenly, at East Russet, Vt., of an old-fashioned Christmas."

The Rise and Fall of the Christmas Card

TWENTY-FIVE years ago (December 21, 1685, to be exact) a man named Ferderber awoke after a week's business trip and realized that he hadn't bought any Christmas presents for his relatives and friends. Furthermore, all he had left from the business trip was eighty cents, two theater-ticket stubs, and a right shoe.

So he cut up some cardboard to fit envelopes and on each card wrote some little thought for the season. Being still a trifle groggy, he thought that it would be nice to make them rhyme although, as he expressed it, with a modest smile, "I am no poet."

The one to his aunt read as follows:

> *"Just a little thought of cheer,*
> *A Merry Christmas and a Happy New Year."*

He liked this one so well that he just copied it on all the others. Then he got excited about the thing and drew a sprig of holly on each card. He mailed them on Christmas Eve and discovered that he still had twenty-eight cents left.

This man Ferderber is now wanted in thirty-two states on the same charge: Starting the Christmas Card Menace. His idea immediately took hold of the public imagination and the next Christmas all his friends and relatives sent

He liked this one so well he just copied it on all the others.

cards to their friends and relatives, for, taking the old lie that "it isn't so much the gift as the spirit i.w.i.i.g." at its face value, they felt that people would be much better pleased with a friendly greeting than a nasty old gift. And, for a while, the custom really was quite a relief.

Then the thing began to get out of hand. Big Christmas card manufacturing concerns sprang up all over the country and factory sites adjacent to freight sidings were at a premium. Millions and millions of cards were printed and millions and millions of people began sending them to each other. Along about December 15, the blight began and, like locusts, the envelopes started drifting in from the mail. Seventy-five thousand extra mail carriers were drafted into service and finally the Government was forced to commandeer all males under 25 who did not have flat feet. Even at that, all the Christmas cards couldn't be delivered until the first of the year, and by that time the flood of New Year's cards had begun, for everyone who received Christmas cards from people to whom they had sent none rushed out and bought New Year's cards to send them the next week, just as if that was what they had intended to do all along.

It became impossible to read all these cards, and finally even to open them. Great stacks of unopened envelopes covered desks and hall tables throughout the country. Some of the wealthier citizens had chutes built on the outside of their houses into which the postmen dumped the cards and by means of which they were conveyed direct to the furnace. The poorer people, unable to convert their mail matter into fuel in this manner, unable sometimes to clear away a path from their front door to the street, often starved to death before their provisions could be got to them. The winter of 1927 was known as the Winter of the Red Death, for all over the country families were snowed in with envelopes and perished before help could be brought to them. In some towns fires were accidentally started with results too horrible to relate.

UNEARTH VALUABLE SCIENTIFIC DATA

Excavators who have recently been at work in the Middle West digging through mounds of petrified envelopes have furnished valuable data on the nature of these *objets d'art*. The most popular design seems to have been that involving a fireplace with stockings hanging from it, with the slogan, evidently satirical, "A Merry Christmas and a Happy New Year." Candles were also highly considered as decoration; candles and bells. When human figures were introduced, they were of the most unpleasant types: short, fat, bearded men dressed in red, offensively gay little children in pajamas carrying lighted candles, stagecoaches filled with steaming travelers, sleigh rides and coasting parties, and street musicians annoying householders with Christmas carols. The text was usually in Old English type, so that fortunately it was difficult, if not impossible, to read.

Evidently the tide began to turn when someone, perhaps a descendant of the very Ferderber who had brought all this distress on the land, thought of the idea of venting his personal spleen in his Christmas cards. He thought that, since no one read them anyway, he might as well say what he really felt, so long as he said it in Old English type. It would be a satisfaction to him, anyway. So near the top of these mounds of Early Twentieth Century cards we find some on this order:

A picture of a holly wreath with a large hammer stuck through it and the following legend:

"Just to Wish You the Measles.
Christmas 1931."

Another showed a little cottage on the brow of a snow-covered hill with the sun setting behind it. On the cottage was a sign: "For Sale." The sentiment underneath was:
> *"Peace on Earth, Good Will Toward Men;*
> *Heh! Heh!"*

This was followed by a period of wide-spread bootlegging.

A New Year's card, with "Greetings" embossed at the top, read:
> *"If I don't see you in 1933*
> *1934 will be soon enough for me."*

As soon as this fad caught on, the pendulum swung the other way. The sentiments, beginning with the mildly abusive, gradually became actually vicious.

We find one, dated 1938, which says:

> *"This Christmas Eve I want you to know,*
> *That if you don't leave $50,000 in Box 115 before*
> *New Year's, I'll sell your letters, you crook, you."*

Another, in a wreath of mistletoe, bore the following explicit legend:

> *"Watch Your Wife."*

It was naturally but a step from these to downright obscene vituperation, and at this point the reform societies stepped in. A campaign was carried on throughout the country, which, unlike other reform campaigns, had the backing of a majority of the public. It was but the work of a year or so to induce the necessary two-thirds of the state legislatures to consent to an amendment to the Constitution forbidding the manufacture and sale of Christmas cards. Naturally this was followed by a period of widespread bootlegging, but it was half-heartedly supported and soon collapsed.

All of which is merely a historical summary of what has been done in the past, preliminary to launching a campaign against the manufacture of all Christmas presents, with the exception of toys. What our fathers did, we can do.

"Greetings From—"

DURING the Christmas and New Year's season there was an ugly rumor going the rounds of the counting-houses and salons (Note to Printer: Only one "o," please!) of the town that I was in jail. I would like to have it understood at this time that I started that rumor myself. I started it, and spent quite a lot of money to keep it alive through the use of paid whisperers, in order that my friends would understand why they got no gifts or greeting cards from me. They couldn't expect a man who was in jail to send them anything. Or could they?

I have now reached an age and arterial condition where this business of selection of gifts for particular people throws me into a high fever (102) and causes my eyes to roll back into my head. It isn't the money that I begrudge. I spend that much in a single night on jaguar cubs and rare old Egyptian wines for one of my famous revels. It is simply that I am no longer able to decide what to get for whom. In other words, that splendid cellular structure once known as my "mind" has completely collapsed in this particular respect. (I am finding other respects every day, but we won't go into that now.)

It is not only at Christmas and New Year's that I am confronted with this terrifying crisis. When I am away on my summer vacation, when I go away on a business trip, or even when I wake up and find myself in another city by mistake, there is always that incubus sitting on my chest: "Which postcard shall I send to Joe?" or "What shall I take back to Mae?" The result is that I have acquired a full-blown phobia for postcard stands and the sight of a gift shop standing in my path will send me scurrying around a three-mile detour or rolling on the ground in an unpleasant frenzy. If I knew of a good doctor, I would go to him for it.

On my last vacation I suddenly realized that I had been away for two weeks without sending any word home other than to cable the bank to mind its own business and let me alone about that overdraft. So I walked up and down in front of a postcard shop until I got my courage up, gritted my teeth, and made a dash for it. I found myself confronted by just short of 450,000 postcards.

Taking up a position slightly to the left and half facing one of those revolving racks, I gave it a little spin once around, just to see if it was working nicely. This brought the lady clerk to my side.

"Some postcards?" she asked, perhaps to make sure that I wasn't gambling with the contraption.

"I'm just looking," I reassured her. Then, of course, I *had* to look. I spun the thing around eighty or ninety times, until it began to look as if there were only one set of postcards in the rack, all showing some unattractive people in a rowboat on a moonlit lake. Then I started spinning in the opposite direction. This made me dizzy and I had to stop altogether. "Let me see," I said aloud to myself in order to reassure the lady that I really was buying cards and not just out on a lark, "who—whom—do I have to send to?"

Well, there were four in my own family, and Joe and Hamilton and Tweek and Charlie (something comical for Charlie)—oh, and Miss McLassney in the office and Miss Whirtle in the outer office and Eddie on the elevator, and then a bunch of kidding ones for the boys at the Iron Gate and—here I felt well enough to start spinning again. Obviously the thing to do was to take three or four dozen at random and then decide later who to send each one to. So I grabbed out great chunks of postcards from the rack, three out of this pack showing mountain goats, six out of this showing a water-colored boy carrying a bunch of pansies (these ought to get a laugh), and seven or eight showing peasants in native costume flying kites or something.

"I'll take these," I said, in a fever of excitement, and dashed out without paying.

For four days I avoided sitting down at a desk to write those cards, but at last a terrific mountain storm drove me indoors and the lack of anything to read drove me to the desk. I took the three dozen cards and piled them in a neat pile before me. Then I took out my fountain pen. By great good luck, there was no ink in it. You can't write postcards without ink, now, can you? So I leapt up from the desk and took a nap unti the storm was over.

It was not until a week later that I finally sat down again and began to decide which cards to send and to whom. Here was one showing an old goat standing on a cliff. That would be good for Joe, with some comical crack written on it. No, I guess this one of two peasant girls pushing a cart would be better for Joe. I wrote, "Some fun, eh, kid?" on the goat picture and decided to send it to Hamilton, but right under it was a colored one showing a boy and girl eating a bunch of lilies of the valley. That would be better for Hamilton—or maybe it would be better

"I'm just looking," I reassured the lady clerk.

for Charlie. No, the goat one would be better for Charlie, because he says "Some fun, eh, kid?" all the time . . . Now let's do this thing systematically. The goat one to Charlie. Cross off Charlie's name from the list. That's one. Now the boy and girl eating lilies of the valley—or perhaps this one of a herd of swans—no, the boy and girl to Hamilton because—hello, what's this? How about *that* for Hamilton? And how about the boy and girl eating a herd of swans in a cartful of lilies of the valley on a cliff for Eddie or Joe or Miss McLassney or Mother or Tweek or—

At this point everything went black before me and when I came to I was seated at a little iron table on a terrace with my face buried in an oddly flavored glass of ice. Not having had a stamp, I didn't send even the card I had written to Charlie, but brought them all home with me in my trunk and they are in my top desk drawer to this very day.

The question of bringing home little gifts is an even more serious one. On the last day before I start back I go to some shop which specializes in odds and ends for returning travelers. I have my list of beneficiaries all neatly made out. Here are some traveling clocks. Everyone *has* a traveling clock. Here are some embroidered hand bags. (As a matter of fact, I have come to believe that the entire choice of gifts for ladies, no matter where you are, is limited to embroidered hand bags. You ask a clerk for suggestions as to what to take to your mother, and she says: "How about a nice embroidered hand bag?" You look in the advertisements in the newspapers and all you can find are sales of embroidered hand bags. The stores at home are full of embroidered hand bags and your own house is full of embroidered hand bags. My God, don't they ever think of anything else to make?)

I roam about in shop after shop, thinking that in the next one I shall run across something that will be just right. Traveling clocks and embroidered hand bags. Perfumes and embroidered hand bags. Perfumes and traveling clocks. And all of them can be bought at home right down on Main Street and probably a great deal better. At this point, the shops all close suddenly, and I am left with my list and lame ankles to show for a final day's shopping. It usually results in my sneaking out, the first day that I am home, and buying a traveling clock, some perfume, and an embroidered hand bag at the local department store and presenting them without the telltale wrappings to only moderately excited friends.

This is why I pretend to be in jail around Christmas and New Year's. It may end up in my pretending to be (or actually being) in jail year the round.

The Stranger Within
Our Gates

ONE of the problems of child education which is not
generally included in books on the subject is the Visiting Schoolmate. By this is meant the little friend whom
your child brings home for the holidays. What is to be
done with him, the Law reading as it does?

He is usually brought home because his own home is in
Nevada, and if he went 'way out there for Christmas he
would no sooner get there than he would have to turn
right around and come back—an ideal arrangement on the
face of it. But there is something in the idea of a child
away from home at Christmas-time that tears at the heart-
strings, and little George is received into the bosom of your
family with open arms and a slight catch in the throat.
Poor little nipper! He must call his parents by telephone on
Christmas day; they will miss him so. (It later turns out
that even when George's parents lived in Philadelphia he
spent his vacation with friends, his parents being no fools.)

For the first day George is a model of politeness.
"George is a nice boy," you say to your son; "I wish you
knew more like him." "George seems to be a very manly
little chap for fourteen," your wife says after the boys have

gone to bed. "I hope that Bill is impressed." Bill, as a matter of fact, does seem to have caught some of little George's gentility and reserve, and the hope for his future which had been previously abandoned is revived again under his schoolmate's influence.

The first indication that George's stay is not going to be a blessing comes at the table, when, with confidence born of one day's association, he announces flatly that he does not eat potatoes, lamb or peas, the main course of the meal consisting of potatoes, lamb and peas. "Perhaps you would like an egg, George?" you suggest. "I hate eggs," says George, looking out the window while he waits for you to hit on something that he does like.

"I'm afraid you aren't going to get much to eat tonight, then, George," you say. 'What is there for dessert?"

"A nice bread pudding with raisins," says your wife.

George, at the mention of bread pudding, gives what is known as "the bird," a revolting sound made with the tongue and lower lip. "I can't eat raisins anyway," he adds, to be polite. "They make me come out in a rash."

"Ah-h! The old raisin-rash," you say. "Well, we'll keep you away from raisins, I guess. And just what is it that you can eat, George? You can tell me. I am your friend."

Under cross-examination it turns out that George can eat beets if they are cooked just right, a rare species of egg-plant grown only in Nevada, and all the ice cream in the world. He will also cram down a piece of cake now and then for manners' sake.

All this would not be so bad if it were not for the fact that, coincidentally with refusing lamb, George criticizes your carving of it. "My father carves lamb across the grain instead of the way you do," he says, a little crossly.

"Very interesting," is your comment.

"My father says that only old ladies carve straight down like that," he goes on.

"Well, well," you say pleasantly between your teeth, "that makes me out sort of an old lady, doesn't it?"

"Perhaps you have a different kind of lamb in Nevada," you suggest, hacking off a large chunk. (You have never carved so badly.) "A kind that feeds on your special kind of eggplant."

"We don't have lamb very often," says George. "Mostly squab and duck."

"You stick to squab and duck, George," you say, "and it will be just dandy for that rash or yours. Here, take this and like it!" And you toss him a piece of lamb which, oddly enough, is later found to have disappeared from his plate.

It also turns out later that George's father can build sail-boats, make a monoplane that will really fly, repair a broken buzzer and imitate birds, none of which you can do and none of which you have ever tried to do, having given it to be understood that they *couldn't* be done. You begin to hate George's father almost as much as you do George.

"I suppose your father writes articles for the magazines, too, doesn't he, George?" you ask sarcastically.

"Sure," says George with disdain. "He does that Sundays—Sunday afternoons."

"Yes, sir," says George.

This just about cleans up George so far as you are concerned, but there are still ten more days of vacation. And during these ten days your son Bill is induced by George to experiment with electricity to the extent of blowing out all the fuses in the house and burning the cigarette-lighter out of the sedan; he is also inspired to call the cook a German spy who broils babies, to insult several of the neighbors' little girls to the point of tears and reprisals, and to refuse spinach. You know that Bill didn't think of these things himself, as he never could have had the imagination.

On Christmas Day all the little presents that you got for George turn out to be things that he already has, only his are better. He incited Bill to revolt over the question of where the tracks to the electric train are to be placed (George maintaining that in his home they run through his father's bathroom, which is the only sensible place for tracks to run). He breaks several of little Barbara's more fragile presents and says that she broke them herself by not knowing how to work them. And the day ends with George running a high temperature and coming down with the mumps, necessitating a quarantine and enforced residence in your house for a month.

This is just a brief summary of the Visiting Schoolmate problem. Granted that every child should have a home to go to at Christmas, could there not be some sort of state subsidy designed to bring their own homes on to such children as are unable to go home themselves? On such a day each home should be a sanctuary, where only members of the tribe can gather and overeat and quarrel. Outsiders just complicate matters, especially when outsiders cannot be spanked.

The presents turn out to be things he already has, only his are better.

Bayeux Christmas
Presents Early

IT SEEMS rather strange that, in the very year which marks the nine hundredth anniversary of the birth of William the Conqueror, a strip of Bayeux tapestry should have been discovered in Bayeux, New Jersey, depicting the passage of that hero across the Channel. It seems so strange, in fact, that the police are investigating the matter.

The tapestry, it is alleged by the defense, shows four of the Conqueror's ships in mid-Channel. There seems to be some doubt among authorities as to the direction in which the ships are going—to or from Albion. We incline to the theory that they are on their way back to France. There must have been at least four boat-loads of Normans who were disappointed in England and who turned right around and went home.

Or, if we must be seasonal, we may hold to the theory that they are on their way back to Normandy for the Christmas holidays. Can you imagine the bustle and din there must have been in William's household along about December 20 of the first Christmas week following the landing? "Going home for Christmas?" must have been the question on all lips framed in probably the worst Norman-

English ever heard. "Noël," they probably called it. The old oaken bucket that hung in Noël—to put it badly.

Any study of a Bayeux tapestry is made difficult by the fact that the old weavers were such bum draughtsmen. They may have known how to work looms but they couldn't draw for a darn. There is no way of telling from the tapestry whether or not William himself was aboard one of the ships, because all the men look alike, if you can even call it that. The man in the middle boat, the one bunking up with a horse, might be William, but the chances are against it. He is evidently so sick that he doesn't care *who* he is. He is making a mental resolution that, rather than cross this Channel again, he will spend the rest of his life in Normandy, or wherever it is he is headed for.

The little boat, which seems to be hanging in mid-air is really, they tell us, in the distance. Its occupants are having a rather thin time of it and are evidently considering being ill, too. On the whole, the entire expedition would have done better never to have left land.

A word about the figureheads on the two ships which have them. The one on the boat at the extreme right would indicate that it is going in the opposite direction from the rest of the fleet, or else that somebody made an awful blunder in assembling the ship. It is on the stern, as near as we can figure it out, although the two boys amidships who are humming together confuse things by facing in opposite directions themselves. Judged merely as figureheads neither one is worth much, although we like the one on the right better than the big one of the left because the latter looks as if the designer had tried to be funny.

We gather that there was some vague idea of having the great black things held by the pilots look like rudders. Well, they don't—and that goes for the whole tapestry, too.

Here Come the Children

MANY parents are confronted this month by the problem of homing children. Just as you have got the house picked up after Thanksgiving, the private schools and colleges let their charges loose again for two or three weeks because of Christmas or some such pretext, and before you know it Spencer and Beth and eight or ten of their little playmates land on you, palpitating for entertainment. What, as the question runs, to do?

There was a time when all you had to do to entertain the kiddies was to string some festoons of red paper from the chandelier to the corners of the table and cry "Surprise, surprise!" when they came into the room. Then perhaps some of those godawful snapping arrangements with paper hats and mottoes concealed inside a percussion cap would throw the young folks into such a state of excitement that they couldn't eat for a week afterward. Those who were able to stand up after this enervating sport were allowed to indulge their sex appetites in a game of "Post Office." And when their parents came for them at a quarter to nine, it was voted that a delirious time had been had and thank you very much, Mrs. Hosmer.

But if you want to hear the merry sound of children's mocking laughter, just try one of those parties on them today. The chances are that they will start throwing rolls and olive pits at you and leave the house with curses on their lips. The children who are coming home from school today for the holidays are built of sterner stuff. They want red meat. The holidays mean to them something like what King Manuel of Portugal used to go off on when he would disappear from home and not show up for ten days.

In view of this change in standards of entertainment, it would perhaps be well to line up a few ways of keeping young folks happy while they are in our midst celebrating the Nativity. For, after all, we must keep in touch with the children, because some day they will get all of Grandma's money.

This is one of the most successful entertainments for boys and girls just home from the exacting confinement of school. It is called a "Paul Jones" party, because Paul Jones was a notorious souse. It was even whispered at one time that he was the father of the American navy, but no one was ever able to prove it.

In order to prepare the house for this party, it will be necessary to take down all the pictures and draperies and move all the furniture out. The corners in every room should be banked and a tarpaulin stretched over the floors.

A lemonade should be prepared, consisting of lemon juice, gin, vermouth, bitters, and a little crushed mint. For the older children something with bacardi is nice, or perhaps, if they are children from the neighborhood whom you know very well, just straight Scotch.

Begin the party at 11:30, which will give them time to go to the theatre first. Do not be discouraged at their scornful air as they enter the house. They are that way to everybody. The lemonade will soon fix that, and before the evening is over they may warm up to the extent of coming over and speaking to you personally.

Paul Whiteman's orchestra should have been imported from New York for the occasion and should be made to play continuously. Nothing short of Paul Whiteman's will do, and if even they aren't playing their best, considerable comment will be elicited from the tiny guests.

After sufficient dancing has been indulged in, the big game of the evening may be suggested. The company is divided into couples and each couple is provided with a high-powered roadster. Starting in relays from the porte-cochère, they should be sent off in different directions. The idea of the game is to see which couple can stay out the longest. The winners will be presented with a marriage license and their flat silver.

Another Uncle Edith Christmas Story

UNCLE Edith said: "I think it is about time that I told you a good old-fashioned Christmas story about the raging sea."

"Aw, nuts!" said little Philip.

"As you will," said Uncle Edith, "but I shall tell it just the same. I am not to be intimidated by a three-year-old child. Where was I?"

"You were over backwards, with your feet in the air, if I know anything about you," said Marian, who had golden hair and wore it in an unbecoming orange ribbon.

"I guess that you probably are right," said Uncle Edith, "although who am I to say? Anyway, I *do* know that we sailed from Nahant on the fourteenth March."

"What are you—French?" asked little Philip, "the fourteenth March."

"The fourteenth *of* March, then," said Uncle Edith, "and if you don't shut up I will keep right on with the story. You can't intimidate me."

"Done and done," said little Philip, who bled quite a lot from a wound in his head inflicted a few seconds before by Uncle Edith.

"We set sail from Nahant on the fourteenth *of* March (nya-a-a-a-a) on the good ship *Patience W. Littbaum*, with a cargo of old thread bound for Algeciras."

"End of story!" announced Marian in a throaty baritone.

"It is *not* the end of the story, and I will sue anyone who says that it is," petulated Uncle Edith. "You will know well enough when I come to the end of the story, because I shall fall over on my face. Now be quiet or Uncle Edith will give you a great big abrasion on the forehead."

"I can hardly wait," said little Philip, or whichever the hell one of those children it was, I can't keep them all straight, they are all so much alike.

"Aboard," continued Uncle Edith, "aboard were myself, as skipper—"

"Skippered herring," (*a whisper*).

"—Lars Jannssenn, first mate; Max Schnirr, second mate; Enoch Olds, third base; and a crew of seven whose names you wouldn't recognize. However, there we were.

Max Schnirr, second mate.

"The first 709 days were uneventful. The sailmaker (a man by the name of Sailmaker, oddly enough) made eleven sails, but, as we had no more ships to put them on, and our sails were O.K., we had to throw them overboard This made the men discontented, and there were rumors of mutiny. I sent a reporter up to see the men, however, and the rumors were unconfirmed; so I killed the story. NO MUTINY was the head I put on it in the ship's paper that night, and everybody was satisfied."

"You great big wonderful animal," said Marian, running her tiny hand through Uncle Edith's hair.

"It was nothing," said Uncle Edith, and everybody agreed that it certainly was.

"However," continued the old salt pork, "everyone on board felt that something was wrong. We were at that time at Lat. seventy-eight, Long. seventy-eight, which cancelled each other, making us right back where we started from—"

"Don't tell me that we are back at Nahant again," said little Philip, throwing up.

"Not exactly Nahant," said Uncle Edith, "but within hailing distance of a Nahanted ship."

"You just used Nahant in the first place so that you could pull that gag," said Primrose, who, up to this time, had taken no part in the conversation, not having been born.

"So help me God," said Uncle Edith, "it came to me like *that!*" And he snapped a finger, breaking it. "The ha'nted ship lay just off our starboard bow, and seemed to be manned by mosquitoes. As we drew alongside, however, we found that there was not a soul on board. Not a soul on board."

"That is the second time you have said that," said little whatever-his-name-is—Philip.

Uncle Edith made no reply other than to throw nasty little Philip into irons.

" 'Prepare to board!' was the order given. And everybody, ignoring the chance for a pun, prepared to board the derelict. In a few seconds we were swarming over the side of the empty ship and searching every nook and cranny of her. The search, however, was fruitless. The ship's log was found in the wheelhouse, but, as the last entry read, 'Fair and warm. Billy said he didn't love me as much as he does Anna' we discarded that as evidence. In the galley we found a fried egg, done on only one side, and an old bo'sun who was no good to anybody. Other that these two things, the mystery was complete."

"Not that I give a damn," said Marian, "but what was

Lars Jannssenn, first mate

the explanation to this almost complete mystery?"

"If you will shut your trap," said Uncle Edith, "I will tell you. As I may not have told you, the mystery ship was full of sleeping Hessian troops, such as were used against the colonists in the Revoluntionary War. They were very gay in their red coats and powdered wigs, and, had they been awake, might have offered some solution of the problem which now presented itself to us.

" 'What shall I do, cap'n?' asked Lars Jannssenn, who had been promoted to purser.

" 'What would you *like* to do, Lars?' I asked him.

" 'Me, I would like to have three wishes,' was the typically Scandinavian reply. (Lars had belonged to the Scandi-navy before he joined up with us.)

" 'They are yours,' I said, more on the spur of the moment than anything else. 'You take your three wishes and put them in your hat and pull it down over your ears. Anybody else?'

"Suddenly there was a scream from below decks. I have heard screams in my day, but never anything like this one. It was dark by now, and there were a lot of couples necking in the lifeboats. But this scream was different. It was nothing human. It came from the bowels of the ship, and you know that's bad.

" 'All hands below!' I cried, and just as everybody was rushing down the hatchways there came a great explosion, seemingly from the jib.

" 'All hands to the jib!' I cried in my excitement.

" 'What is all this—a game?' asked the crew, as one man.

" 'I am captain here,' I said, boxing the compass roundly, 'and what I say goes! In the future please try to remember that fact.'

"Well, this sort of thing went on for hours. Up and down the ship we went, throwing overboard Hessians in our rush, until finally the cook came to me and said: 'Cap'n, I frankly am sick of this. Are there, or there not, any reasons why we should be behaving like a pack of schoolboys?'

"This was a poser. I called the crew together and we decided to go back to the *Patience W. Littbaum*. But, on looking over the side, we found a very suspicious circumstance. *The Patience W. Littbaum was gone!*"

"I don't believe it!" said little Philip, from the brig.

Uncle Edith turned sharply, "I thought you were in irons," he said.

"You think a lot," replied little Philip, and the entire casino burst into gales of laughter, although it was a pretty lousy come-back, even for a three-year old.

"Very well, then," said Uncle Edith, "I am sorry if you feel that way. For I was just going to end the story by saying that we sailed the mystery ship back to Nahant."

"And where does Christmas come in?" piped up Marian, who hadn't heard a word of Uncle Edith's story.

"Who the hell said anything about Christmas?" asked Uncle Edith in a rage.

And who the hell did?

Home for the Holidays

As a pretty tribute to that element of our population which is under twenty-two years of age, these are called "the Holidays".

This is the only chance that the janitors of the schools and colleges have to soak the floors of the recitation halls with oil to catch the dust of the next semester, and while this is being done there is nothing to do with the students but to send them home for a week or two. Thus it happened that the term "holidays" is applied to that period of the year when everybody else is working just twice as hard and twice as long during the week to make up for that precious day which must be lost to the Sales Campaign or the Record Output on Christmas Day.

For those who are home from school and college it is called, in the catalogues of their institutions, a "recess" or "vacation," and the general impression is allowed to get abroad among the parents that it is to be a period of rest and recuperation. Arthur and Alice have been working so hard at school or college that two weeks of good quiet home-life and home cooking will put them right on their feet again, ready to pitch into that chemistry course in which, owing to an incompetent instructor, they did not do very well last term.

That the theory of rest during vacation is fallacious can be proved by hiding in the coat closet of the home of any college or school youth home for Christmas recess. Admission to the coat closet may be forced by making yourself out to be a government official or an inspector of gas meters. Once hidden among the overshoes, you will overhear the following little earnest drama, entitled "Home for the Holidays."

There was a banging of the front door, and Edgar has arrived. A round of kisses, an exchange of health reports, and Edgar is bounding upstairs.

"Dinner in half an hour," says Mother.

"Sorry," shouts Edgar from the bathtub, "but I've got to go out to the Whortleberrys' to a dinner dance. Got the bid last week. Say, have I got any dress-studs at home here? Mine are in my trunk."

Father's studs are requisitioned and the family cluster at Edgar's door to slide in a few conversational phrases while he is getting the best of his dress shirt.

"How have you been?" (Three guesses as to who it is that asks this.)

"Oh, all right. Say, have I got any pumps at home? Mine are in the trunk. Where are those old ones I had last summer?"

"Don't you want me to tie your tie for you?" (Two guesses as to who it is that asks this.)

"No, thanks. Can I get my laundry done by tomorrow night? I've got to go out to the Clamps' at Short Neck for over the week-end to a bobsledding party, and when I get back from there Mrs. Dibble is giving a dinner and theater party."

"Don't you want to eat a little dinner here before you go yo the Whortleberrys'?" (One guess as to who it is that asks this.)

But Edgar has bounded down the stairs and left the Family to comfort each other with such observations as "He looks tired," "I think that he has filled out a little," or "I wonder if he's studying too hard."

You might stay in the coat-closet for the entire two weeks and not hear much more of Edgar than this. His parents don't. They catch him as he is going up and down stairs and while he is putting the studs into his shirt, and are thankful for that. They really get into closer touch with him while he is at college, for he writes them a weekly letter then.

Nerve-racking as this sort of life is to the youth who is supposed to be resting during his vacation, it might be even more wearing if he were to stay within the Family precincts. Once in a while one of the parties for which he has been signed up falls through, and he is forced to spend an evening at home. At first it is somewhat embarrassing to be thrown in with strangers for a meal like that, but, as the evening wears on, the ice is broken and things assume a more easy swing. The Family begins to make remarks.

"You must stand up straighter, my boy," says Father, placing his hand between Edgar's shoulderblades. "You are slouching badly. I noticed it as you walked down the street this morning."

"Do all the boys wear soft-collared shirts like that?" asks Mother. "Personally, I think that they look very untidy. They are all right for tennis and things like that, but I wish you'd put on a starched collar when you are in the house. You never see Elmer Quiggly wearing a collar like that. He always looks neat."

"I can remember you when you were that high."

"For heaven's sake, Eddie," says Sister, "take off that tie. You certainly do get the most terrific-looking things to put around your neck. It looks like a Masonic apron. Let me go with you when you buy your next batch."

By this time Edgar has his back against the wall and is breathing hard. What do these folks know of what is being done?

If it is not family heckling it may be that even more insidious trial, the third degree. This is usually inflicted by semi-relatives and neighbors. The formulae are something like this:

"Well, how do you like your school?"

"I suppose you have plenty of time for pranks, eh?"

"What a good time you boys must have! It isn't so much what you get out of books that will help you in after life, I have found, but the friendships made in college. Meeting so many boys from all parts of the country—why, it's a liberal education in itself."

"What was the matter with the football team this season?"

"Let's see, how many more years have you? What, only one more! Well, well, and I can remember you when you were that high, and used to come over to my house wearing a little green dress, with big mother-of-pearl buttons. You certainly were a cute little boy, and used to call our cook 'Sna-Sna.' And here you are, almost a senior."

"Oh, I wonder if you know a fellow named—er— Mellish—Spencer Mellish? I met him at the beach last summer. I am pretty sure that he is in your class—well, no, maybe he's only a sophomore."

After an hour or so of this, Edgar is willing to go back to college and take an extra course in Blacksmithing, Chipping and Filing, given during the Christmas vacation, rather than run the risk of getting caught again. And, whichever way you look at it, whether he spends his time getting into and out of his evening clothes, or goes crazy answering questions and defending his mode of dress, it all adds up to the same in the end—fatigue and depletion and what the doctor would call "a general run-down nervous condition."

The younger you are the more frayed you get. Little Wilbur comes home from school, where he has been put to bed at 8:30 every night with the rest of the fifth form boys, and has had to brush his hair in the presence of the headmaster's wife, and dives into what might be called a veritable maelstrom of activity. From a diet of cereal and fruit-whips, he is turned loose in the butler's pantry among the maraschino cherries and given free rein at the various children's parties, where individual pound-cake Santas and brandied walnuts are followed by an afternoon at "Treasure Island," with the result that he comes home and insists on tipping every one in the family the black spot and breaks the cheval glass when he is denied going to the six-day bicycle race at two in the morning.

Little girls do practically the same, and, if they are over fourteen, go back to school with the added burden of an *affaire de coeur* contracted during the recess. In general, it takes about a month or two of good, hard schooling and overstudy to put the child back on its feet after the Christmas rest at home.

Which leads us to the conclusion that our educational system is all wrong. It is obvious that the child should be kept at home for eight months out of the year and sent to school for the vacations.

Holiday! Holiday!

A Christmas Story

THE hot sun beat down on the Plaza. Little Miguel O'Rourke felt terrible. Those *huijos!* That old *caballerizo!* He should never have touched them. They were not meant for little boys five years old. But on the night before the Feast of Seven Mittens one must do something, even if it is only to kill one's uncle and throw his legs away. August was the month of the Feast of the Seven Mittens, and August is the month of love the world over.

Suddenly Miguel was awakened by a rough shout, and looking behind him he saw a lumberjack who had evidently lost his way. The poor thing was so frightened that he was darting back and forth, not knowing whether he was afoot, horseback, or good red herring. Lumberjacks usually live in Maine, you know, and here it was nearly half-past eight.

"Where are you going, Doctor Melcher?" asked Miguel. Miguel always called strangers "Doctor Melcher" because it was Doctor Melcher who had once given him that nasty medicine.

The rough old lumberjack looked down at the little boy. "Wa-a-ll, pardner," he said, "I ain't much on sentiment, as you ought to know by this time, but it just kinder seemed to me that I ought to bring something to Little Wheel-Dust, the golden-haired daughter of my old side-kick who was left with me for dead that night eleven years ago in the old shack in Calgary." So saying, the old miner pulled out of his pocket a tiny torpedo with "I Love You" painted on it. "It's for Little Wheel-Dust," he said simply, and fainted.

Now this way a trying situation for a young lad of Miguel O'Rourke's age, whatever it was. To be left with a torpedo would be bad enough, but to have an old lumberjack lying in the hot sun of the Plaza was unthinkable. And on St. Valentine's Day, too!

"Wa-a-ll, pardner, I ain't much on sentiment."

Little Miguel sat sorrowfully by the tiny pile of faded flowers which had once been men like himself. "Thanksgiving," he murmured. "I wish I had some cozy home to go to on this day of all days. I wish I had some turkey."

Hardly had he spoken when with a great swish a rug appeared before him on which was seated a little old man in the uniform of a Chief Petty Officer.

"I have just heard your wish, Little Orson," he said.

"Little Miguel," corrected Miguel.

"Little Miguel," said the C.P.O. "My mother's name was Orson," he explained, "Ruth Orson; and every Eastertide I find myself calling people 'Orson'."

"That's quite all right," said Miguel; "my mother's name was Ruth Orson, too, so I know how it is." And he smiled a crooked little smile.

"I have just heard your wish, Orson," continued the little old man, "your wish that you might have a Thanksgiving turkey, and so I hopped on my rug right away to come and tell you that we haven't got a turkey left in the house. How about a little roast-beef? It's very nice today."

"I would love some roast-beef," said Miguel, "if you will see to it that all the pits are taken out first. I choked on a pit once."

"Before we go," said the C.P.O., "I want you to make sure that you are dressed warmly enough. Remember what day it is, and in all your merrymaking don't forget that you are alive and happy today because one hundred and fifty years ago now your great-great-grandfather and his brave associates met in Philadelphia and drew up that document which was to establish liberty in America and insure you and me against tyranny from the English king. I think that the least we can do before opening up the bottle is to bow our heads and think very hard for three minutes on the bravery and devotion of Amerigo Vespucci."

And, as they stood with tears streaming down their little faces, suddenly a clash and clang of chimes rang out on the frosty air and the glorious cadence of *Integer Vitae* filled their very being with its grandeur.

"A Merry Christmas," said the little old man.

"And a Merry Christmas to *you*, too," said Little Miguel. *Clash—clang! Clash—clang!*

"My mother's name was Ruth Orson, too."

A Christmas Spectacle

*For Use in Christmas Eve Entertainments
in the Vestry*

AT the opening of the entertainment the Superintendent will step into the footlights, recover his balance apologetically, and say:

" 'Boys and girls of the Intermediate Department, parents and friends: I suppose you all know why we are here to-night. (At this point the audience will titter apprehensively.) Mrs. Drury and her class of little girls have been working very hard to make this entertainment a success, and I am sure that everyone here tonight is going to have what I overheard one of my boys the other day calling 'some good time.' (Indulgent laughter from the little boys.) And may I add before the curtain goes up that immediately after the entertainment we want you all to file out into the Christian Endeavor room, where there will be a Christmas tree, 'with all the fixin's,' as the boys say." (Shrill whistling from the little boys and immoderate applause from everyone.)

There will then be a wait of twenty-five minutes, while sounds of hammering and dropping may be heard from behind the curtains. The Boys' Club orchestra will render the "Poet and Peasant Overture" four times in succession, each time differently.

At last one side of the curtains will be drawn back; the other will catch on something and have to be released by hand; someone will whisper loudly, "Put out the lights," following which the entire house will be plunged into darkness. Amid catcalls from the little boys, the footlights will at last go on, disclosing:

The windows in the rear of the vestry rather ineffectively concealed by a group of small fir trees on standards, one of which has already fallen over, leaving exposed a corner of the map of Palestine and the list of gold-star classes for November. In the center of the stage is a larger tree, undecorated, while at the extreme left, invisible to everyone in the audience except those sitting at the extreme right, is an imitation fireplace, leaning against the wall.

Twenty-five seconds too early little Flora Rochester will prance out from the wings, uttering the first shrill notes of a song, and will have to be grabbed by eager hands and pulled back. Twenty-four seconds later the piano will begin "The Return of the Reindeer" with a powerful accent on the first note of each bar, and Flora Rochester, Lillian McNulty, Gertrude Hamingham and Martha Wrist will swirl on, dressed in white, and advance heavily into the footlights, which will go out.

There will then be an interlude while Mr. Neff, the sexton, adjusts the connection, during which the four little girls stand undecided whether to brave it out or cry. As a compromise they giggle and are herded back into the wings by Mrs. Drury, amid applause. When the lights go on again, the applause becomes deafening, and as Mr. Neff walks triumphantly away, the little boys in the audience will whistle: "There she goes, there she goes, all dressed up in her Sunday clothes!"

"The Return of the Reindeer" will be started again and the show-girls will reappear, this time more gingerly and somewhat dispirited. They will, however, sing the following, to the music of the "Ballet Pizzicato" from "Sylvia":

> "We greet you, we greet you,
> On this Christmas Eve so fine.
> We greet you, we greet you,
> And wish you a good time."

They will then turn toward the tree and Flora Rochester will advance, hanging a silver star on one of the branches, meanwhile reciting a verse, the only distinguishable words of which are: *"I am Faith so strong and pure —"*

At the conclusion of her recitation, the star will fall off.

Lillian McNulty will then step forward and hang her star on a branch, reading her lines in clear tones:

> *"And I am Hope, a virtue great,*
> *My gift to Christmas now I make,*
> *That children and grown-ups may hope today*
> *That tomorrow will be a merry Christmas Day."*

The hanging of the third star will be consummated by Gertrude Hamingham, who will get as far as *"Sweet Charity I bring to place upon the tree—"* at which point the strain will become too great and she will forget the remainder. After several frantic glances toward the wings, from which Mrs. Drury is sending out whispered messages to the

effect that the next line begins, *"My message bright —"*
Gertrude will disappear, crying softly.

After the morale of the cast has been in some measure
restored by the pianist, who, with great presence of mind,
plays a few bars of "Will There Be Any Stars In My
Crown?" to cover up Gertrude's exit, Martha Wrist will un-
leash a rope of silver tinsel from the foot of the tree, and,
stringing it over the boughs as she skips around in a circle,
will say, with great assurance:

> " *'Round and 'round the tree I go,*
> *Through the holly and the snow*
> *Bringing love and Christmas cheer*
> *Through the happy year to come."*

At this point there will be a great commotion and jangling of sleigh-bells off-stage, and Mr. Creamer, rather
poorly disguised as Santa Claus, will emerge from the opening in the imitation fireplace. A great popular demonstra-
tion for Mr. Creamer will follow. He will then advance to
the footlights, and, rubbing his pillow and ducking his
knees to denote joviality, will say thickly through his false
beard:

"Well, well, well, what have we here? A lot of bad little
boys and girls who aren't going to get any Christmas
presents this year? (Nervous laughter from the little boys
and girls.) Let me see, let me see! I have a note here from
Dr. Whidden. Let's see what it says. (Reads from a paper
on which there is obviously nothing written. 'If you and
the young people of the Intermediate Department will come
into the Christian Endeavor room, I think we may have a

"'Round and 'round the tree I go."

little surprise for you . . .' Well, well, well! What do you suppose it can be? (Cries of "I know, I know!" from sophisticated ones in the audience.) Maybe it is a bottle of castor-oil! (Raucous jeers from the little boys and elaborately simulated disgust on the part of the little girls.) Well, anyway, suppose we go out and see? Now if Miss Liftnagle will oblige us with a little march on the piano, we will all form in single file —"

At this point there will ensue a stampede toward the Christian Endeavor room, in which chairs will be broken, decorations demolished, and the protesting Mr. Creamer badly hurt.

This will bring to a close the first part of the entertainment.

The King and
The Old Man

Being a Whimsical Legend, Written without
Apologies to the London Christmas Weeklies

FOR you must know that in those days there was a King ruling the land who was very great, so great even that he was called "Pepin Glabamus," or "Pepin Flatfoot," and there were in his kingdom anywhere from twenty-and-four to twenty-and-eight maidens who were in sore distress and concerning whom no one, not even the youth of the university, had any interest whatsoever. Now the King grieved greatly at this, and so great was his grief that he became known far and wide as "Pepin Glubabo" or "Pepin Red-Eye." He was also known as "That Old Buzzard."

Now there came to the castle one night an Old Man, who begged admittance on the grounds that he represented the Fuller Brush Company and would like to show the King a thing or two about brushing. But the King, who was still in high dudgeon (the low dudgeons being full of paynims and poor white trash left over from the Fifth, or Crucial, Crusade), sent out word that he had already been brushed and to get the hell out from under that portcullis.

But the Old Man paid no heed to the King's command,
but instead sent back word that he had some very nice
mead which was guaranteed to make the drinker's ears fly
out and snap back, all to the count of "one-two-one-two."
So the King, it being Christmas Eve and being sorely trou-
bled in spirit, sent down word, "Oh, well." And so the
Old Man came up.

And so the Old Man came up. (A very medieval and
mystic effect is gained by repeating the same sentence
twice, as you will find out by reading farther in this tale,
you sucker.) And when he had reached the King's chamber,
he encountered the Chamberlain who, lest the Queen
should take to prowling of a night, was always stationed by
the door in possession of a loud gong and a basket of red
fire. And, at the sound of the gong and the sight of the
red fire over the transom, the King was accustomed to
open a secret passageway like a flash, and into this secret
passageway could dart any business friends who might be
sharing a friendly nightcap with His Majesty. Only one
night, being sore confused and in something of a daze, the
King himself had darted into the secret passageway, leaving
the business friend behind on top of the silken canopy, very
uncomfortable from the pointed spearheads which held the
canopy in place. It was from this unhappy incident, or so
said the jester and court winchell, that the Royal Museum
acquired its rare collection of golden tresses and slightly
damaged neck ornaments, listed in the catalogue under the
head of "Or Else."

At last the Old Man came into the presence of the King
and, what with opening his sack of mead and testing it
himself (the King being no fool), and what with giving of
it to the King for him to taste, and what with trying it
first with juice of half a lemon and then with effervescent

waters to see which way it went best, it was no time at all before both the King and the Old Man were going through the King's supply of neckties to see which ones they should send to the Pope for Christmas.

"Here is one that I have worn only once," said the King.

"How did you ever happen to do that?" asked the Old Man, looking at its tapestry design and screaming with laughter.

And the King screamed, too, not once but eleven times—and the evening was on. The evening was on, and the night was on, and the morning, up until ten-thirty, was on, and, by that time, the Queen was on and had packed up and gone to her mother's.

And so it happened that late on Christmas Day the King rolled over and, finding his head where it had bounced under the bed, replaced it on one shoulder and rubbed his eyes, which he found in the pocket of his waistcoat, and then said:

"Old Man, who *are* you?"

But the Old Man had gone on, rather, it looked to the King as if he had gone, but he was all the time in the open bureau drawer with the neckties.

And so, to this day, no one ever found out who the Old Man really was, but there are those who say that he was the West Wind, and there are those who say that he was the Down from a Thistle, but there are older and wiser ones who say that he was just a naughty Old Man.

A Christmas Pantomime

For Kiddies and Grown-Ups, or Neither

*T*he scene is on a snowy plain just outside Wilkes-Barre. The characters in this pantomime are:

PIERROT ....A pierrot
COLUMBINE ....A pierrot
CIBOULETTE...A pierrot
RINTINTIN...A pierrot
LITTLE LAURA ....*who dreams the dream.*

As the curtain rises, something goes wrong; so it has to be lowered again. Twenty-five minute wait while it is fixed.

As the curtain rises, Pierrot *is discovered sneaking a drink out of a bottle. He puts the bottle down quickly when he finds out that he has been discovered.*

Enter Columbine, *awkwardly. She dances over to* Pierrot *and makes as if to kiss him; but he hits her a terrific one under the eye and knocks her cold. Three thousand gnomes enter and drag her off. One gnome (Alaska) stays behind and dances a little.*

END OF THE SHOW: EVERYBODY OUT!

On thinking it over, a Christmas pantomime doesn't seem to be just what is needed. You can get a Christmas pantomime anywhere. In fact, *don't* you? So let's not do a Christmas pantomime. Let's just have some fun and get to bed early.

Let's tell some Yuletide stories!

I know a good Christmas story. It seems there was a man who came to a farmer's house late on Christmas Eve and asked if the farmer could put him up for the night.

"Ich habe kein Zimmern," sagte der Farmer, "aber Sie können mit Baby schlafen." ("I have no rooms," said the farmer, "but you may sleep with the baby if you wish.") So the man —

I guess that isn't about Christmas, though. You can tell it as if it were about Christmas, however, by putting that in about it's being Christmas Eve when the man came to the farm-house. But it really wasn't Christmas Eve in the original story and I couldn't deceive you.

Games are good on Christmas Eve. I know some good games. One that we used to play when I was a boy was called "Bobbing for Grandpa." All you need is a big tub full of water, or gin, and a grandfather. Grandpa gets into the tub and ducks his head under the water. Then everyone steals softly out of the room and goes to the movies. You ought to be back by eleven-fifteen at the latest. Then you all rush into the room, pell-mell, and surprise the old gentleman.

Oh, I don't know but what the pantomime was best, after all. You can get more of the spirit of Christmas into a pantomime. Let's go back and do some more of that old pantomime. You surely remember the pantomime?

Ciboulette *enters carrying a transparency which reads:* "This is Christmas and You Are Going to Be Merry, and Like It, Too . . . Toyland Chamber of Commerce." *She dances around a bit and finally finds a good place to exit, which she does, thank God!*

Pierrot *awakes and sees his image in the pool. He goes right back to sleep again.*

This brings every character on except Rintintin *and there doesn't seem to be any good reason for bringing him on at all. However, he insists and comes on, dancing across the stage to where* Pierrot *is sitting. This cleans up the entire cast and after* Pierrot *has danced around the sleeping* Columbine *once or twice, something in the manner of a dying rose-bud, which he claims to represent, the curtains come together again and we are left flat, with only about half of our Christmas Eve over and nothing more to do before bedtime.*

Heigh ho! Perhaps we can get Mr. Rodney to tell us some ghost stories. Mr. Rodney, please!

Mr. Rodney: Well, children. Here it is Christmas Eve and no one has pulled the Christmas Carol yet. If you will all draw up close and stop your necking, I will at least start . . . Stop, there is someone at the door. You answer, Alfred, it's probably for you.

Alfred: No, Mr. Rodney, it's a little old man in a red coat and a white beard who says he's Santa Claus.

Mr. Rodney: Send for the police. I'll Santa Claus him.

At this moment, Santa Claus *himself enters. He is a tall, thin man, with black side-whiskers, and wears a raincoat and a derby.*

Santa Claus: My name is Mortimer, George Pearson Mortimer. A lot of silly people call me "Santa Claus" and it makes me pretty mad, I can tell you. Santa Claus, indeed! Just because one year, a long time ago, I got a little stewed and hired a sleigh and some reindeer and drove around town dropping presents down chimneys. I was arrested at the corner of State and Market streets and when they took me to the station-house I didn't want to give my right name; so I gave "Santa Claus" and thought it very funny. The trouble *that* got me into!

Mr. Rodney: Do you mean to tell us that there is no such person as Santa Claus?

Santa Claus: Yes—or rather no!

(Mr. Rodney *bursts into tears.*)

Mr. Rodney stops crying to listen. "Hark, what is that?" he says.

"It's the sun on the marshes, Mr. Rodney," they all say in unison and the curtain comes down on the final scene of the pantomime.

In this scene, Pierrot comes to life again and revisits the old haunts of his boyhood where he used to spend Christmas years and years ago. First he comes to the old Christmas turkey, which is much too old by now for any fun. Then he sees the Little Girl That He Used to Play With in His Holidays. She is now the mother of three children and engaged to be married. But still Pierrot seems dissatisfied. He is very evidently looking for something, searching high and low. First he looks in his vest pockets, then in his coat pockets. Finally he looks in his trousers pockets. But whatever it is, he cannot find it.

"What are you looking for?" asks Ciboulette, voicing the sentiments of the entire gathering.

"I can't seem to remember where I put the check the coat room girl gave me for my hat and coat," he answers. "I could swear that I put it right in here with my old theatre-ticket stubs."

"I didn't give you any check," says the coat room girl. "I know your face."

Pierrot *laughs at his mistake as*
THE CURTAIN FALLS.

Editha's Christmas Burglar

IT was the night before Christmas, and Editha was all agog. It was all so exciting, so exciting! From her little bed up in the nursery she could hear Mumsey and Daddy downstairs putting the things on the tree and jamming her stocking full of broken candy and oranges.

"Hush!" Daddy was speaking. "Eva," he was saying to Mumsey, "it seems kind of silly to put this ten-dollar gold-piece that Aunt Isaac sent to Editha into her stocking. She is too young to know the value of money. It would just be a bauble to her. How about putting it in with the house-hold money for this month? Editha would then get some of the food that was bought with it and we would be ten dollars in."

Dear old Daddy! Always thinking of someone else! Editha wanted to jump out of bed right then and there and run down and throw her arms about his neck, perhaps shutting off his wind.

"You are right, as usual, Hal," said Mumsey. "Give me the gold-piece and I will put it in with the house funds."

"In a pig's eye I will give you the gold-piece," replied Daddy. "You would nest it away somewhere until after Christmas and then go out and buy yourself a muff with it. I know you, you old grafter." And from the sound which followed, Editha knew that Mumsey was kissing Daddy. Did ever a little girl have two such darling parents? And, hugging her Teddy-bear close to her, Editha rolled over and went to sleep.

*   *   *   *   *

She awoke suddenly with the feeling that someone was downstairs. It was quite dark and the radiolite traveling-clock which stood by her bedside said eight o'clock, but, as the radiolite traveling-clock hadn't been running since Easter, she knew that that couldn't be the right time. She knew that it must be somewhere between three and four in the morning, however, because the blanket had slipped off her bed, and the blanket always slipped off her bed between three and four in the morning.

And now to take up the question of who it was downstairs. At first she thought it might be Daddy. Often Daddy sat up very late working on a case of Scotch and at such times she would hear him downstairs counting to himself. But whoever was there now was being very quiet. It was only when he jammed against the china-cabinet or joggled the dinner-gong that she could tell that anyone was there at all. It was evidently a stranger.

Of course, if might be that the old folks had been right all along and that there really was a Santa Claus after all, but Editha dismissed this supposition at once. The old folks had never been right before and what chance was there of their starting in to be right now, at their age? None at all. It couldn't be Santa, the jolly old soul!

It must be a burglar then! Why, to be sure! Burglars always come around on Christmas Eve and little yellow-haired girls always get up and go down in their nighties and convert them. Of course! How silly of Editha not to have thought of it before!

With a bound the child was out on the cold floor, and with another bound she was back in bed again. It was too cold to be fooling around without slippers on. Reaching down by the bedside, she pulled in her little fur foot-pieces which Cousin Mabel had left behind by mistake the last time she visited Editha, and drew them on her tiny feet. Then out she got and started on tip-toe for the stairway.

She did hope that he would be a good-looking burglar and easily converted, because it was pretty gosh-darned cold, even with slippers on, and she wished to save time.

As she reached the head of the stairs, she could look down into the living-room where the shadow of the tree stood out black against the gray light outside. In the doorway leading into the dining room stood a man's figure, silhouetted against the glare of an old-fashioned burglar's lantern which was on the floor. He was rattling silverware. Very quietly, Editha descended the stairs until she stood quite close to him.

"Hello, Mr. Man!" she said.

"Hello, Mr. Man!" she said.

The burglar looked up quickly and reached for his gun.

"Who the hell do you think you are?" he asked.

"I'se Editha," replied the little girl in the sweetest voice she could summon, which wasn't particularly sweet at that as Editha hadn't a very pretty voice.

"You's Editha, is youse?" replied the burglar. "Well, come on down here. Grandpa wants to speak to you."

"Youse is not my Drandpa," said the tot, getting her baby and tough talk slightly mixed. "Youse is a dreat, bid burglar."

"All right, kiddy," replied the man. "Have it your own way. But come on down. I want ter show yer how yer kin make smoke come outer yer eyes. It's a Christmas game."

"This guy is as good as converted already," thought Editha to herself. "Right away he starts wanting to teach me games. Next he'll be telling me I remind him of his little girl at home."

So with a light heart she came the rest of the way downstairs, and stood facing the burly stranger.

"Merry Christmas to all and to all a goodnight."

"Sit down, Editha," he said, and gave her a hearty push which sent her down heavily on the floor. "And stay there, or I'll mash you one on that baby nose of yours."

This was not in the schedule as Editha had read it in the books, but it doubtless was this particular burglar's way of having a little fun. He *did* have nice eyes, too.

"Dat's naughty to do," she said, scoldingly.

"Yeah?" said the burglar, and sent her spinning against the wall. "I guess you need attention, kid. You can't be trusted." Whereupon he slapped the little girl. Then he took a piece of rope out of his bag and tied her up good and tight, with a nice bright bandana handkerchief around her mouth, and trussed her up on the chandelier.

"Now hang there," he said, "and make believe you're a Christmas present, and if you open yer yap, I'll set fire to yer."

Then, filling his bag with the silverware and Daddy's imitation sherry, Editha's burglar tip-toed out by the door. As he left, he turned and smiled. "A Merry Christmas to all and to all a Good Night," he whispered, and was gone.

And when Mumsey and Daddy came down in the morning, there was Editha up on the chandelier, sore as a crab. So they took her down and spanked her for getting out of bed without permission.

The Young Folks' Day

A Child's-eye View of the Whole Thing

STEPHEN is two and a half, and has certain very definite reasons for wanting to complete the process of slipping an old iron washer over the stem of a broken Ingersoll watch. He has been working on it in his crib since five o'clock in the morning, and here it is barely six-thirty when the Head of the House comes in, dressed very unbecomingly in bath robe and slippers, and says, with forced gaiety:

"Well now, sir, how about going downstairs and seeing what Santa has brought?"

There has been a lot of talk about this "Santa" for several weeks past, none of it particularly interesting. It seems that he comes down the chimney or something, obviously a falsehood. And even if he does, what of it?

However, the Head of the House and his Wife appear to derive a great deal of innocent merriment out of talking about the event; so it is best to humor them and simulate an interest.

This is a bit too thick, though, to be dragged away from important work with the iron washer and taken downstairs on a purely speculative hunt after what this "Santa" may or may not have brought. It has been emphasized in the preliminary conversations on the subject that this "jolly old soul" reserves considerable leeway to himself in the question of whether or not certain boys are to receive any presents at all, the whole thing being contingent on whether or not they have been what is technically known as "good boys" during the two weeks previous. A glance back at Stephen's behavior during the past two weeks convinces him that his chances are hardly worth while getting out of bed to go downstairs for.

There is no other way, however, as he is picked up bodily (a cowardly thing for a great big bully like the Head of the House to do, simply because he has the size) and carried downstairs to where a large, brilliantly lighted tree is standing by the fireplace. A tree in the house is ridiculous in the first place, but there is unquestionably something nice about those lights. Do you suppose that by squeezing one of them the color could be made to ooze out into the hand, and from there be transferred to the face, like marmalade or paints? Well, there is no way to find out like trying, so here goes.

"No, no, Stephen! Mustn't touch lights!" (Why *will* these people insist on leaving out definite articles when talking to anyone ten years younger than they are? Do they think it makes it any easier to understand them? They just make fools of themselves, that's all.) "Here, see this dreat big booful doggie that Santa brought Stephen!" (Sickening, isn't it?)

The "dreat big booful doggie" turns out to be a flat failure. It is too big, to begin with. Then, too, there is nothing about it with a hole in it, like that washer (by the way, where *is* that washer?) which can be slipped over the stem of the Ingersoll. In this world, everything stands or falls by its ability to be slipped over the stem of the Inger-soll.

Then the Head of the House drags out a sort of mechanical banjo-player which you wind up and watch jump. The

He is picked up bodily and carried downstairs.

Head of the House thinks it is great. He winds it up and then says, "Look at that, will you, Doris!" Stephen tries to have a go at it, but it appears that it must be wound up by some older person. And if you can't wind a thing up yourself, what is the sense in fooling with it at all?

"Well, I guess Santa Claus was pretty good to you," says a neighbor who has come in to see Stephen with his toys. "I just love to watch their faces when they see all the new things," she says. Anyone watching Stephen's face, however, would detect nothing more inspiriting than a slight expression of disgust at the Head of the House making such a show of himself over the mechanical banjo-player.

This goes on for some time, a line of grown-ups stepping up and waving some new inanity in Stephen's face and saying, "Oh, look, 'Teven!" (Another one calling him " 'Teven" is going to get a good swift bust in the face) and then retiring to play with it themselves.

There are two things left in the world that Stephen wants to do. One is to try pinching those lights. And the other is to finish slipping the old iron washer over the stem of the Ingersoll. The lights are out of the question now, but not the washer. All you have to do is crawl very quietly up the stairs and down the hall (the mechanical toys are making so much noise that no one will notice you) and there, on the floor, is the best little toy that God ever made. That, man, is a *toy!*

And now to get down to work with it. After all, Christmas was meant for the grown-ups. The rest of us have things to do.

Christmas Afternoon

Done in the Manner, if Not the Spirit, of Dickens

WHAT an afternoon! Mr. Gummidge said that, in his estimation, there never had *been* such an afternoon since the world began, a sentiment which was heartily endorsed by Mrs. Gummidge and all the little Gummidges, not to mention the relatives who had come over from Jersey for the day.

In the first place, there was the *ennui*. And such *ennui* as it was! A heavy, overpowering *ennui*, such as results from a participation in eight courses of steaming, gravied food, topping off with salted nuts which the little old spinster Gummidge from Oak Hill said she never knew when to stop eating—and true enough she didn't—a dragging, devitalizing *ennui*, which left its victims strewn about the livingroom in various attitudes of prostration suggestive of those of the petrified occupants in a newly unearthed Pompeiian dwelling; an *ennui* which carried with it a retinue of yawns, snarls and thinly veiled insults, and which ended in ruptures in the clan spirit serious enough to last throughout the glad new year.

Then there were the toys! Three and quarter dozen toys to be divided among seven children. Surely enough, you or

I might say, to satisfy the little tots. But that would be because we didn't know the tots. In came Baby Lester Gummidge, Lillian's boy, dragging an electric grain-elevator which happened to be the only toy in the entire collection which appealed to little Norman, five-year-old son of Luther, who lived in Rahway. In came curly-headed Effie in frantic and throaty disputation with Arthur, Jr., over the possession of an articulated zebra. In came Everett, bearing a mechanical negro which would no longer dance, owing to a previous forcible feeding by the baby of a marshmallow into its only available aperture. In came Fonlansbee, teeth buried in the hand of little Ormond, who bore a popular but battered remnant of what had once been the proud false-bosom of a hussar's uniform. In they all came, one after another, some crying, some snapping, some pulling, some pushing—all appealing to their respective parents for aid in their intra-mural warfare.

And the cigar smoke! Mrs. Gummidge said that she didn't mind the smoke from a good cigarette, but would they mind if she opened the windows for just a minute in order to clear the room of the heavy aroma of used cigars? Mr. Gummidge stoutly maintained that they were good cigars. His brother, George Gummidge, said that he, likewise, would say that they were. At which colloquial sally both the Gummidge brothers laughed testily, thereby breaking the laughter record for the afternoon.

Aunt Libbie, who lived with George, remarked from the dark corner of the room that it seemed just like Sunday to her. An amendment was offered to this statement by the cousin, who was in the insurance business, stating that it was worse than Sunday. Murmurings indicative of as hearty agreement with this sentiment as their lethargy would allow came from the other members of the family circle, causing

Mr. Gummidge to suggest a walk in the air to settle their dinner.

And then arose such a chorus of protestations as has seldom been heard. It was too cloudy to walk. It was too raw. It looked like snow. It looked like rain. Luther Gummidge said that he must be starting along home soon, anyway, bringing forth the acid query from Mrs. Gummidge as to whether or not he was bored. Lillian said that she felt a cold coming on, and added that something they had had for dinner must have been undercooked. And so it went, back and forth, forth and back, up and down, and in and out, until Mr. Gummidge's suggestion of a walk in the air was reduced to a tattered impossibility and the entire company glowed with ill-feeling.

In the meantime, we must not forget the children. No one else could. Aunt Libbie said that she didn't think there was anything like children to make a Christmas; to which Uncle Ray, the one with the Masonic fob, said, "No, thank God!" Although Christmas is supposed to be the season of good cheer, you (or I, for that matter) couldn't have told, from listening to the little ones, but what it was the children's Armageddon season, when Nature had decreed that only the fittest should survive, in order that the race might be carried on by the strongest, the most predatory and those possessing the best protective coloring. Although there were constant admonitions to Fonlansbee to "Let Ormond have that whistle now; it's his," and to Arthur, Jr., not to be selfish, but to "give the kiddie-car to Effie; she's smaller than you are," the net result was always that Fonlansbee kept the whistle and Arthur, Jr., rode in permanent, albeit disputed, possession of the kiddie-car. Oh, that we mortals should set ourselves up against the inscrutable workings of Nature!

What an afternoon!

Hallo! A great deal of commotion! That was Uncle George stumbling over the electric train, which had early in the afternoon ceased to function and which had been left directly across the threshold. A great deal of crying! That was Arthur, Jr., bewailing the destruction of his already useless train, about which he had forgotten until the present moment. A great deal of recrimination! That was Arthur, Sr., and George fixing it up. And finally a great crashing! That was Baby Lester pulling over the tree on top of himself, necessitating the bringing to bear of all of Uncle Ray's knowledge of forestry to extricate him from the wreckage.

And finally Mrs. Gummidge passed the Christmas candy around. Mr. Gummidge afterward admitted that this was a tactical error on the part of his spouse. I no more believe that Mrs. Gummidge thought they wanted that Christmas candy than I believe that she thought they wanted the cold turkey which she later suggested. My opinion is that she wanted to drive them home. At any rate, that is what she succeeded in doing. Such cries as there were of "Ugh! Don't let me see another thing to eat!" and "Take it away!" Then came hurried scramblings in the coat-closet for overshoes. There were the rasping sounds made by cross parents when putting wraps on children. There were insincere exhortations to "come and see us soon" and "get together for lunch some time." And, finally, there were slammings of doors and the silence of utter exhaustion, while Mrs. Gummidge went about picking up stray sheets of wrapping paper.

And, as Tiny Tim might say in speaking of Christmas afternoon as an institution, "God help us, every one."

Uncle Edith's Ghost Story

"TELL us a ghost story, Uncle Edith," cried all the children late Christmas afternoon when everyone was cross and sweaty.

"Very well, then," said Uncle Edith, "it isn't much of a ghost story, but you will take it—and like it," he added, cheerfully. "And if I hear any whispering while it is going on, I will seize the luckless offender and baste him one.

"Well, to begin, my father was a poor wood-chopper, and we lived in a charcoal-burner's hut in the middle of a large, dark forest."

"That is the beginning of a fairy story," cried little Dolly, a fat, disagreeable child who never should have been born, "and what we wanted was a *ghost* story."

"To be sure," cried Uncle Edith, "what a stupid old woopid I was. The ghost story begins as follows:

"It was late in November when my friend Warrington came up to me in the club one night and said: 'Craige, old man, I want you to come down to my place in Whoopshire for the week-end. There is greffle shooting to be done and grouse no end. What do you say?'

"I had been working hard that week, and the prospect

pleased. And so it was that the 3:40 out of Charing Cross found Warrington and me on our way into Whoopshire, loaded down with guns, plenty of flints, and two of the most beautiful snootfuls every accumulated in Merrie England.

"It was getting dark when we reached Breeming Downs, where Warrington's place was, and as we drove up the shadowy path to the door, I felt Warrington's hand on my arm.

" 'Cut that out!' I ordered peremptorily. 'What is this I'm getting into?'

" 'Sh-h-h!' he replied, and his grip tightened. With one sock I knocked him clean across the seat. There are some things I simply will not stand for.

"He gathered himself together and spoke. 'I'm sorry,' he said. 'I was a bit unnerved. You see, there is a shadow against the pane in the guest room window.'

" 'Well, what of it?' I asked. It was my turn to look astonished.

"Warrington lowered his voice. 'Whenever there is a shadow against the windowpane as I drive up with a guest, that guest is found dead in bed the next morning—dead from fright,' he added, significantly.

"I looked up at the window toward which he was pointing. There, silhouetted against the glass, was the shadow of a gigantic man. I say 'a man,' but it was more the figure of a large weasel except for a fringe of dark-red clappers that it wore suspended from its beak."

"How do you know they were dark red," asked little Tom-Tit, "if it was the shadow you saw?"

"You shut your face," replied Uncle Edith. "I could

hardly control my astonishment at the sight of this thing, it was so astonishing. 'That is in my room?' I asked Warrington.

" 'Yes,' he replied, 'I am afraid that it is.'

"I said nothing, but got out of the automobile and collected my bags. 'Come on,' I announced cheerfully, 'I'm going up and beard Mr. Ghost in his den.'

"So up the dark, winding stairway we went into the resounding corridors of the old seventeenth-century house, pausing only when we came to the door which Warrington indicated as being the door to my room. I knocked.

"There was a piercing scream from within as we pushed the door open. But when we entered, we found the room empty. We searched high and low, but could find no sign of the man with the shadow. Neither could we discover the source of the terrible scream, although the echo of it was still ringing in our ears.

" 'I guess it was nothing,' said Warrington, cheerfully. 'Perhaps the wind in the trees,' he added.

" 'But the shadow on the pane?' I asked.

"He pointed to a fancily carved piece of guest soap on the washstand. 'The light was behind that,' he said, 'and from outside it looked like a man.'

" 'To be sure,' I said, but I could see that Warrington was as white as a sheet.

" 'Is there anything that you need?' he asked. 'Breakfast is at nine—if you're lucky,' he added, jokingly.

" 'I think that I have everything,' I said. 'I will do a little reading before going to sleep, and perhaps count my laundry . . . But stay,' I called him back, 'you might leave that revolver which I see sticking out of your hip pocket. I may need it more than you will.'

"He slapped me on the back and handed me the revolver as I had asked. 'Don't blow into the barrel,' he giggled, nervously.

" 'How many people have died of fright in this room?' I asked, turning over the leaves of a copy of *Town and Country*.

" 'Seven,' he replied. 'Four men and three women.'

" 'When was the last one here?'

" 'Last night,' he said.

" 'I wonder if I might have a glass of hot water with my breakfast,' I said. 'It warms your stomach.'

" 'Doesn't it though?' he agreed, and was gone.

"Very carefully I unpacked my bag and got into bed. I placed the revolver on the table by my pillow. Then I began reading.

"Suddenly the door to the closet at the farther end of the room opened slowly. It was in the shadows and so I could not make out whether there was a figure or not. But nothing appeared. The door shut again, however, and I could hear footfalls coming across the soft carpet toward my bed. A chair which lay between me and the closet was upset as if by an unseen shin, and, simultaneously, the window was slammed shut and the shade pulled down. I looked, and there, against the shade, as if thrown from the *outside*, was the same shadow that we had seen as we came up the drive that afternoon."

"I have to go to the bathroom," said little Roger, aged six, at this point.

"Well, go ahead," said Uncle Edith. "You know where it is."

"I don't want to go alone," whined Roger.

"Go with Roger, Arthur," commanded Uncle Edith, "and bring me a glass of water when you come back."

"And whatever was this horrible thing that was in your room, Uncle Edith?" asked the rest of the children in unison when Roger and Arthur had left the room.

"I can't tell you that," replied Uncle Edith, "for I packed my bag and got the 9:40 back to town."

"That is the lousiest ghost story I have ever heard," said Peterkin.

And they all agreed with him.

At Last a Substitute for Snow

WHILE rummaging through my desk drawer the other night I came upon a lot of old snow. I do not know how long it had been there. Possibly it was a memento of some college prank long forgotten. But it suddenly struck me what a funny thing snow is, in a way, and how little need there really is for it in the world.

And then I said to myself, "I wonder if it would not be possible to work up some sort of mock snow, a substitute which would satisfy the snow people and yet cause just as much trouble as real snow." And that, my dears, is how I came to invent "Sno."

As you know, real snow is a compound of hydrogen, oxygen, soot, and some bleaching agent. (There is a good bleaching agent who has an office in Room 476, Mechanics' Bank Building. He was formerly General Passenger Agent for the Boston & Maine Railroad, but decided that bleaching was more fun. As a matter of fact, his name is A. E. Roff, or some such thing.)

Again, as you know, real snow is formed by the passage of clouds through pockets of air which are lighter than the air itself, if such a phenomenon were possible. That is to say, these clouds (A) passing through these air-pockets (C) create a certain atmospheric condition known as a "French vacuum." This, in turn, creates a certain amount of ill-feeling, and the result is what we call "snow," or, more often, what we call "this lousy snow."

Now in figuring out what I would have to do to concoct a mock snow, it was necessary to run over in my mind the qualities of snow as we know it. What are the characteristic functions of snow?

Well, first, to block traffic. Any adequate substitute for snow must be of such a nature that it can be applied to the streets of a city in such a way as to tie up all vehicular movement for at least two days. "This," I thought, "requires distribution." Our new snow must be easily and quickly distributed to all parts of town. This will necessitate trucks, and trucks will necessitate the employment of drivers. *Now*, if the weather is cold (and what good is snow unless the weather is cold enough to make it uncomfortable?) these drivers (B) will have to have mittens. So mittens are the first thing that we must get in the way of equipment . . . And I took a piece of paper and wrote down "Mittens." This I crossed out and in its place I wrote "Mittens" again. So far, so good.

Next, one of the chief functions of real snow is to get up in under the cuffs to your sleeves and down inside the collar to your overcoat. Here was a tough one! How to work up something which could be placed up the sleeves and inside the overcoat-collars of pedestrians without causing them the inconvenience of stopping and helping the process. For no substitute for snow could ever be popular which called for any effort on the part of the public. The public wants all the advantages of a thing. Oh, yes! But it doesn't want to go to any trouble to get them. Oh, no! No trouble! If it is going to have snow up its sleeves and in its collars, it wants it put there while it is walking along the street, and no stopping to unbutton or roll back.

So it was evident that, if this function of snow was to be imitated, it would be necessary to hire boys to run along beside people and tuck the substitute in their sleeves and collars as they walked. One boy could perhaps tuck two hundred handsful in an afternoon, and when you figure out the number of people abroad on a good snowy afternoon, you will realize the enormous number of boys it would take to do the job. Girls would be even worse, because they would stop to talk with people.

The problem of distribution thus unsuccessfully met with, the next thing was to decide what other attribute our "Sno" should have that would give it a place in the hearts of millions of snow-lovers throughout the country. Someone suggested "wetness" and in half a second the cry had been taken up in all corners of the conference-room (for we were in conference by now), "Wetness! Wetness! Our 'Sno' must be wet!"

It was decided that the place in which we should have to simulate wetness the most was under bedroom windows. Who does not remember getting up to shut the bedroom windows and stepping into a generous assortment of snowflakes in their prettiest form of disintegration—water? Or even into a drift 'way, 'way out in the middle of the room right where Daddy could slip in it on his way to and from the office? This is perhaps the most difficult feature to imitate — this bedroom drifting, and if, in addition to getting our composition snow into bedroom windows, we could manage some appliance whereby it could be shot into the folds of whatever underclothing might be lying on the chair nearest the window, then indeed might we cry "Eureka!"

The way in which we decided on the name "Sno" for our product would make a story all in itself. The copyright laws forbid one from naming anything "Snow" or "Gold" or "Rolls-Royce," or any noun. This law was passed by some fanatics who took advantage of our boys being away at war to plunge the country into an orgy of blue laws.

. . . hire boys to run along beside people to tuck the substitute in their sleeves.

However, we have no other curse than to abide by the code as it stands.

We therefore decided that, by dropping the *W*, we could make a word which would sound almost like the real word and yet evade the technical provisions on the law. Some of the backers held out for a dressier-sounding name, like

"Flakies" or "Lumpps," but our advertising man, who specializes on Consumer Light Refractions, told us that the effect of a word like "Sno" on the eye of the reader would telegraph a more favorable message to his brain than that of a longer word ending in "ies" or "umpps." Look at the word "Ford," for instance. The success of the Ford product is almost entirely due to the favorable light refractions of the name on the consumer's retina.

This decided us on the trade-name "Sno" and left nothing more for us to do but work out the actual physical make-up of the product and the sort of package to put it out in. The package is also an important feature of any merchandising scheme, and it was decided that a miniature snow-show would be appropriate and rather smart for our particular article. If we could work out some way in which "Sno" could be wrapped up in a six-inch snow-shoe it would not only give the dealer something snappy to display, but would make a nicer-looking package for the consumer to take home—nicer-looking than a snootful of Scotch, for example. You would be surprised, however, to find how difficult it is to wrap up a unit of imitation snow in a snow-shoe, unless you put them both in a box together.

And now all that remains to divulge is the physical make-up of "Sno." That is what we are working on now.

A New Day

GOOD news has just come crashing in through the medium of an old camel with a news-ticker on his back. There is probably going to be an extra day added onto the end of the year, a day especially designed for starting fresh. It is to be called "Year-End Day."

The World Calendar Association (whom Heaven defend!) has a scheme whereby each year begins on a Sunday. This, in itself, is a good idea, as New Year's Eve should always come on Saturday night. Those cauliflower heads look mighty silly on a Tuesday or Thursday morning, wagging themselves to the office.

The plan is to divide the year into quarters (don't ask me how), with the first month of each quarter having thirty-one days and the rest thirty. There are a lot of points yet to be explained to me, but I am being a good sport about waiting.

Anyway, at the end of each year will come an extra day, a sort of loose Saturday banging around between the final Saturday and New Year's Day, and this is to be known as "Year-End Day." On it, you may do whatever you want. Oh, boy, eh?

Just think what you could do with a "Year-End Day"! Break geranium pots, tear up aprons, squirt water through your teeth, and raise Old Ned generally. Compared with such a day, New Year's Eve would seem like the night before your Chemistry Exam.

Or, you could use Year-End Day to recover from New Year's Eve and thereby really start fresh on New Year's Day, instead of having to wait until January 2nd before being able to get your feet into your shoes or to focus on the middle distance.

There are lots of things that I am planning to do on Year-End Day that I have never got around to doing before. One of the first of them will be to get the whole Year-End business straight in my mind. I still don't quite get the hang of it.